RICE PADDIES

AN OFFICIAL'S HOUSE

PEOPLE PAYING THEIR TAXES
WITH RICE TO THE
SHOGUN'S OFFICIAL

KOI, JAPANESE GOLDFISH

To

Dale and Brittany

Debrah
Norise
Lattimore

The FOOL and the PHOENIX

A TALE OF OLD JAPAN

Deborah Nourse Lattimore

JOANNA COTLER BOOKS

An Imprint of HarperCollins*Publishers*

Under the pear blossom moon a poor birdcatcher named Hideo watched a hawk circling overhead. If he caught it, the villagers in the valley below would trade rice to own it. With a silent sweep of his net, Hideo caught the bird. He felt his own heart beat fiercely as the creature struggled in his grasp.

No sooner had Hideo come
to a clearing in the forest than
did a bandit ride down upon him,
knocking him into a shallow ditch.
As Hideo stood up and brushed
himself off, he caught a glimpse
of the bandit's forehead; over
one eyebrow was a deep scar. For
months there had been talk of a
bandit in the mountains, a bandit
who stole from the shogun himself.
Hideo was grateful he had only
been knocked down and not killed.

When Hideo arrived in the
village, people came to look at
the hawk. Then Nobu, head of
the village council, appeared.

"Where did you get that
hawk?" he shouted at Hideo. "It
has a silk cord around its leg."

Hideo looked at Nobu,
then pointed back toward the
mountains.

"Answer me, you!" shouted
Nobu.

"He cannot speak, Lord
Nobu," said the farmer. "He is
the voiceless one from the
mountains."

"Ah!" grunted Nobu. "A fool!
A bad omen to have around!"

"It was just yesterday that word came from the shogun's palace that a prize hunting hawk was missing, along with a treasure and some ponies, too," said a farmer. "Surely if word gets back to the shogun that this fool was seen here with a prize hawk, soldiers will come and burn our village to the ground!"

"Get out of here!" shouted Nobu, shoving Hideo toward the road.

Hideo stopped and looked hard at Nobu. He seemed familiar.

"What are you looking at, you fool? Go on!" yelled Nobu. "Never come back, or it will be your death!"

Hideo trudged away from the village. At the fork in the road near the forest, he released the brilliant black hawk. Perhaps there would be no rice to eat tonight, but the bird would be free.

Alone and hungry, Hideo lay down beneath a spreading pine tree. The sweet sounds of the wind stirring the needles lulled Hideo to sleep. But all of a sudden something stirred in the boughs. In an instant Hideo threw his net. Something was in it! Hideo pulled and pulled. It twisted and wrestled against him.

"Oh! Please! Set me free!" said a soft, trembling voice. "Let me go and I will reward you!"

Hideo dropped the net. Gently and slowly he pushed aside the branches above his head. A dazzling, golden light burst through the needles. The air was heavy with the fragrance of cinnamon and incense. Hideo staggered back and stopped. In the midst of the light was a beautiful maiden. Her robe shimmered in silks of every color, over which lay a garment of golden feathers. Her strange and delicate face turned to Hideo and struck love in the birdcatcher's heart. For a while, neither Hideo nor the maiden moved. At last she spoke.

"Very few mortals ever see me or my kind," said the maiden. "The last to come this way was a bandit, and he killed my husband. Since then I have waited here alone and afraid. You have spared me, and I owe you my life. What wish can I grant you, birdcatcher?"

But Hideo could ask for nothing. He hung his head down in silence. The maiden seemed to read his thoughts.

"No, you are right. I cannot restore your voice," said the maiden. "Stay with me but a while, and neither of us shall be lonely."

She clapped her hands, and an evening meal spread upon golden plates lay at Hideo's feet. And as Hideo began to eat, the maiden sang soft, sweet songs.

It seemed to Hideo to be the longest, most wondrous day of his life, and yet, without his realizing it, a whole month had passed. For him there was no day or night or loneliness or hunger.

But the day came when noises entered the forest, noises Hideo knew to be the shogun's men searching for something or someone. *The bandit!* Hideo thought. *No one has found him. If he is not found soon, and the shogun's treasure is not returned, the village will be burned to the ground!* As the soldiers passed below on the forest path, Hideo slowly covered his mouth and tears fell from his eyes. And the maiden again read his thoughts.

"This is the day you must leave me," said the maiden. "For although you and I love each other, only you can save the village. Find the bandit who killed my husband and who not only steals you from me, but also steals the very life from the village."

Then the maiden plucked a single golden feather from her gown and placed it in Hideo's cupped palm. Though it shone with fiery flames, it did not burn. When Hideo looked up, the maiden was gone.

Hideo tied the feather to a thread and put it around his neck. Then he set off for the village. He stopped at the forest's edge. Something was wrong. Where was the sound of the rushing stream that filled the rice paddies in the valley? Walking on, Hideo saw that the streambed was dry, blocked by a large log. Hideo pushed against the log with all his strength until it turned and twisted into the flowing water. In minutes, the stream was full and fat and rushing downhill. *There are many ways to steal the life from a village,* he thought. The feather around his neck glowed.

On Hideo walked toward the valley and the village below. He did not go far when he came upon more wood cuttings and logs. This time they were blocking a pond filled with fat, red fish. *Why, the village ponds must be empty of fish,* he thought. And, as before, Hideo pushed away the logs and branches. And as before, the feather glowed, but this time it was brighter.

On Hideo walked, but soon his path was almost completely blocked. He had to climb over logs and branches scattered all around what seemed to be the opening of a cave. Leaning against a great stone outcropping he looked closer. He could just make out the sounds of horses' whinnies. *The stolen treasure!* he thought. Through a small opening in the brush he saw that he was right. The glitter of gold and silken fabrics was everywhere, and just beyond casks filled with jewels stood a string of handsome horses and racing ponies, nervously pawing the ground.

Hideo ran. The feather around his neck glowed brighter and brighter, and by the time Hideo arrived in the village, the feather was nearly a flame.

Angry farmers stood beside the dried rice paddies and empty fishponds. Among them was Nobu, who turned and stared at Hideo.

"Look!" a farmer shouted. "It is the fool!" And he shook his fist at Hideo.

"Perhaps he is to blame for our misfortune. No water, no fish, and the shogun's men are coming, too."

But before Hideo could get anyone's attention, water rushed into the ponds and they were brimming with fish. The farmers jumped back in amazement, and then they all looked at Hideo. Nobu, too, looked at Hideo. He saw the brilliant flame of gold that the feather was.

"What kind of sorcery is this?" he demanded, his face turning red with anger.

But Hideo stared fixedly at the scar over one of Nobu's eyebrows. Suddenly he remembered where he had seen Nobu before. Nobu was the bandit! Nobu, wise leader of the council, the one who spoke for all, was a thief!

"Get him!" yelled Nobu. "Kill him! The fool is the bandit! See, he wears part of the treasure around his neck!"

The crowd yelled and shoved; some moved with Nobu. Hideo held the feather close. *How can I tell them?* he thought desperately. Without knowing why, Hideo turned and ran toward the forest. The farmers followed, and with them came Nobu. They passed the flowing fishpond. They followed the racing stream. Up higher and higher into the forest they all went, until they came to the spreading pine tree where Hideo had first found the beautiful maiden.

Dozens of hands fell upon Hideo and held him tightly. Nobu stepped forward, a knife in his hand. The tree branches broke apart and a stream of golden light flooded the sky. The beautiful maiden appeared.

"Ah!" she cried, looking at Nobu. "That is the bandit! He is the one who killed my husband, the Phoenix, the bird of prosperity! It was he who almost destroyed your village, too!"

The villagers set Hideo free and grabbed Nobu instead, who, in his shame, confessed what he had done. The villagers begged Hideo to return with them, to live in the village and to serve on the council of the wise. And for a moment Hideo thought he might. But when he remembered the joy he felt beneath the great pine tree, under the gentle gaze of the strange and beautiful maiden, Hideo decided to stay in the woods.

No one in the valley ever saw Hideo again. But from that day on the village prospered. Many, many years after the treasure was returned to the shogun, the ninth Lord of Owari, and the tenth followed him, and his son, and son's son after him, a family walking on the forest path noticed a great, spreading pine tree. Its magnificent boughs and rich, green needles sheltered them from the afternoon sun. But suddenly it glowed, as if it were burning with fire. The frightened family ran back, still watching. Within the golden flames they thought they saw two phoenixes, their wings entwined around each other. Then, with a burst of light, the fire burned out and only ash remained. As suddenly as the fire died, the two phoenixes flew up and out of the ashes, out, over the tops of the trees, over the mountains of Owari, their golden wings beating as one.

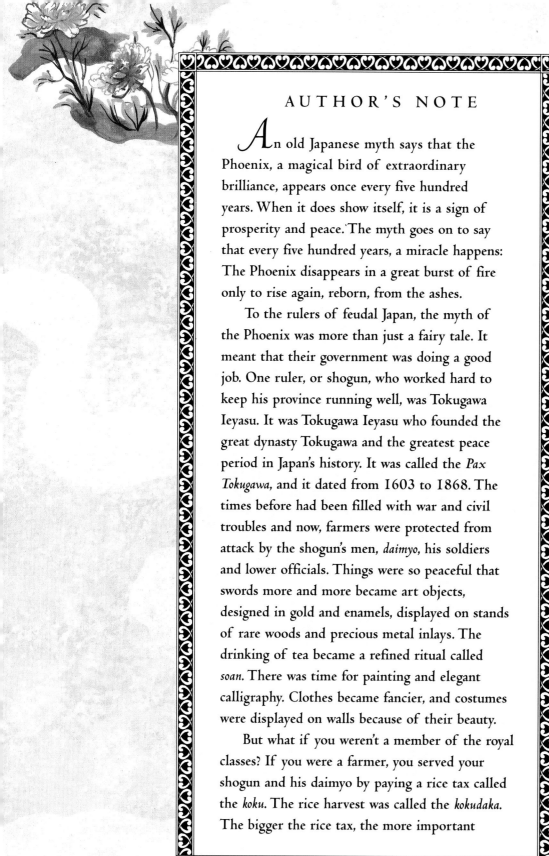

AUTHOR'S NOTE

An old Japanese myth says that the Phoenix, a magical bird of extraordinary brilliance, appears once every five hundred years. When it does show itself, it is a sign of prosperity and peace. The myth goes on to say that every five hundred years, a miracle happens: The Phoenix disappears in a great burst of fire only to rise again, reborn, from the ashes.

To the rulers of feudal Japan, the myth of the Phoenix was more than just a fairy tale. It meant that their government was doing a good job. One ruler, or shogun, who worked hard to keep his province running well, was Tokugawa Ieyasu. It was Tokugawa Ieyasu who founded the great dynasty Tokugawa and the greatest peace period in Japan's history. It was called the *Pax Tokugawa*, and it dated from 1603 to 1868. The times before had been filled with war and civil troubles and now, farmers were protected from attack by the shogun's men, *daimyo*, his soldiers and lower officials. Things were so peaceful that swords more and more became art objects, designed in gold and enamels, displayed on stands of rare woods and precious metal inlays. The drinking of tea became a refined ritual called *soan*. There was time for painting and elegant calligraphy. Clothes became fancier, and costumes were displayed on walls because of their beauty.

But what if you weren't a member of the royal classes? If you were a farmer, you served your shogun and his daimyo by paying a rice tax called the *koku*. The rice harvest was called the *kokudaka*. The bigger the rice tax, the more important

the lands they represented were. One of the shogun's sons collected 620,000 *koku*, or three million bushels of rice a year! If the rice taxes were not paid, even if the rice crops failed, terrible things could happen: Farmers could be punished; officials would be jailed; villages might be destroyed.

Did everyone in the Tokugawa era of Japan like the way things worked? Most probably did. But what if an official in a small town visited the capital at Edo and saw for himself how rich the shogun was? What if he saw the stables of beautiful horses, the aviaries of hunting falcons with their caps and leg ropes of pure silk, and the rich clothing, jewels and furnishings the shogun owned? Might a small-town official become jealous? This is the premise on which my story is based.

This fascinating period of time in Japan's long and rich history produced 20,000 works of art which are now housed in a museum in Japan. The paintings show earlier battles in great detail, how the shogun's men wore heavy armor, how the shogun himself wore a suit of grand armor with metal plates covering his face and body, how swords and arrows and assaults of armies lead to a great period of peace and prosperity.

Against this backdrop of the Tokugawa dynasty, I entered in with a tale of my own. There are many tales from this brilliant civilization; some are known, some are not. Mine is told by a man, Hideo, who cannot even speak. But as he travels through the golden clouds of the richest dynasty in Japan's history, he will find his own path to the Phoenix. May you find yours, too.

—Deborah Nourse Lattimore

To Joanna Cotler

The Fool and the Phoenix
A Tale of Old Japan
Copyright © 1997 by Deborah Nourse Lattimore
Printed in the U.S.A. All rights reserved.

Library of Congress Cataloging-in-Publication Data
Lattimore, Deborah Nourse.
  The fool and the Phoenix : a tale of old Japan / by Deborah Nourse Lattimore.
     p.   cm.
  "Joanna Cotler books."
  Summary: With the help of a mysterious maiden, a mute birdcatcher saves a village
from the plundering of a sly bandit.
  ISBN 0-06-026209-5. — ISBN 0-06-026211-7 (lib. bdg.)
  [1. Robbers and outlaws—Fiction.   2. Japan—Fiction.]   I. Title.
PZ7.L36998Fo   1997   96-27329
[Fic]—dc20   CIP
                                                                                   AC

Typography by Christine Kettner
1   2   3   4   5   6   7   8   9   10
❖
First Edition

Visit the HarperCollins Children's Books web site
http://www.harperchildrens.com